SISTER CiTiES

▲▲▲▲▲▲▲▲▲▲▲▲▲

In a World of Difference

LESLIE BURGER

DEBRA L. RAHM

L

LERNER PUBLICATIONS COMPANY

MINNEAPOLIS

Text copyright © 1996 by Leslie Burger and Debra L. Rahm

All rights reserved. International copyright secured. No part of this book
may be reproduced, stored in a retrieval system, or transmitted in any
form or by any means, electronic, mechanical, photocopying, recording,
or otherwise, without the prior written permission of Lerner Publications
Company, except for the inclusion of brief quotations in an
acknowledged review.

Library of Congress Cataloging-in-Publication Data

Burger, Leslie.
    Sister cities in a world of difference / by Leslie Burger and Debra L. Rahm.
        p.   cm. — (International cooperation series)
    Includes index.
    ISBN 0-8225-2697-2
    1. United States — Relations — Foreign countries — Juvenile
literature. 2. Sister cities — Juvenile literature. I. Rahm, Debra L.
II. Title. III. Series.
    E840.2.B87 1996
    303.48'2 — dc20   95-3424

Manufactured in the United States of America
1 2 3 4 5 6 – JR – 01 00 99 98 97 96

CONTENTS

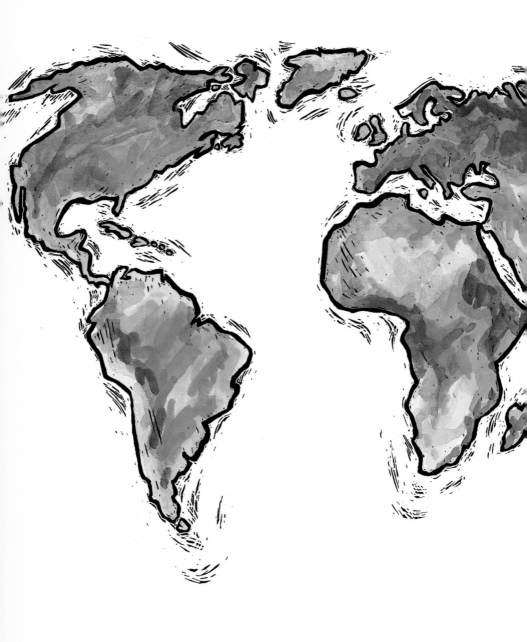

What Are Sister Cities?

The people of the world form a rich tapestry in which hundreds of ways of life are woven together. They live in cities, in small towns, and on farms. They live in the mountains, near oceans, and on the plains. They are rich and poor. They practice different religions and speak different languages.

People everywhere are so different, you may even think you have nothing in common with many of them. If so, you might be surprised. Students everywhere worry about their grades. They like to play games. They're concerned about pollution and crime. They love their families. By learning about each other, people can

These street signs in Los Angeles point to that city's sisters.

Sisters of Los Angeles

- ◆ Athens, Greece
- ◆ Auckland, New Zealand
- ◆ Berlin, Germany
- ◆ Bombay, India
- ◆ Bordeaux, France
- ◆ Eilat, Israel
- ◆ Giza, Egypt
- ◆ Guangzhou, China
- ◆ Jakarta, Indonesia
- ◆ Kaunas, Lithuania

- ◆ Lusaka, Zambia
- ◆ Makati, Philippines
- ◆ Mexico City, Mexico
- ◆ Nagoya, Japan
- ◆ Pusan, Korea
- ◆ St. Petersburg, Russia
- ◆ Salvador, Brazil
- ◆ Taipei Municipality, Taiwan
- ◆ Tehran, Iran
- ◆ Vancouver, Canada

sister city programs got started, how cities become sisters, how they help each other, and how you can get involved. You'll learn about sister city programs in which
young adults have made friends from other countries
and learned about other cultures. You'll see what many
people of all ages have done to help and understand
one another.

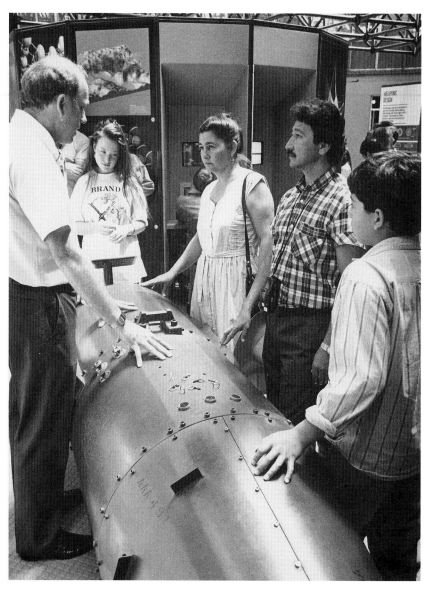

Chaperones and students from Bukhara and from Santa Fe visited a science museum near Santa Fe together, where this replica of an atomic bomb is on display. By choosing to become sisters, their communities are helping to build international understanding— and to lessen the chance that such weapons are used.

Chapter One

Sisters for Peace

Communities become sisters with various goals in mind. Perhaps one of the most important is the goal of peace. The story of **Santa Fe** in the United States and **Bukhara** in the Republic of Uzbekistan (ooz BECK ih STAN) shows how two cities joined specifically to promote peace.

For many years, war threatened to break out between the United States and the former Soviet Union, or USSR. Many concerned people sought ways to avoid it.

Amy Bunting, a woman from Santa Fe, New Mexico, was one of them. "In the early 1980s, both superpowers were terrorizing each other with threats of nuclear destruction," she said. "Many of us felt that a way to avoid this possibility would be for ordinary people in each country to get to know each other."

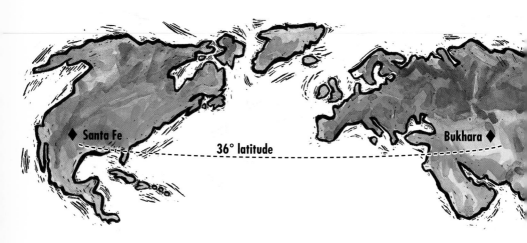

Two Sisters for Peace

Bunting began to "dream of having a sister city in the USSR." She explained, "The idea of a sister city was a natural outgrowth of curiosity about them and a desire to tell them about us."

Many other citizens of Santa Fe felt the same way. They began to search for a city in the Soviet Union that could become their sister. In 1986, they finally found Bukhara—a city on the other side of the world, yet sharing much in common with Santa Fe.

Bukhara (boo HAR ah) is a city of 240,000 people in central Asia. It was part of the Soviet Union until 1991. That year, the Soviet Union ceased to exist as a unified country; it broke into many, smaller countries. One of them is the Republic of Uzbekistan, where Bukhara is located.

The people of Santa Fe selected Bukhara because of its similarities to their own community. The chairman of the Santa Fe Sister City Association, Hilbert Sabin, pointed out some of them. "Both cities are at 36 degrees latitude," he said. "Both are in desert country. Both have ancient traditions of adobe." (Adobe is a type of construction using mud bricks.) Because both cities are in the desert, they are able to grow crops only with the help of their irrigation systems. Both are known for their beautiful weavings—Bukhara for its brilliantly colored silk fabrics and Santa Fe for its woven wool rugs and tapestries.

Bukhara's history goes back 2,500 years, to when it was a trading center on the Silk Road, a main route for merchants traveling from China to the Middle East. Over half its people live in the old part of town, which is about 1,000 years old.

These Bukharan girls showed one visitor from Santa Fe their colorful traditional costumes.

Among the narrow streets and mud dwellings of this old section, some Bukharans still observe ancient customs. The city includes many ethnic groups, including Tadzhik (tahd JEEK), Turkmen, Tartar, Slav, and Jewish peoples.

Like Bukhara, Santa Fe was also on a major trading route. From 1821 to 1880, it was at the end of the Santa Fe Trail, a pioneer route across part of the western and southwestern United States. The city, located in the midst of many Indian pueblos, was founded by the Spanish as a trading center in 1609. Santa Fe is still an important center for arts and crafts. Like Bukhara, its people come from many ethnic groups. Although people of all races and ethnic backgrounds live in Santa Fe, the city has three main groups: Hispanics (people whose ancestors came from Spain or Mexico), Anglos (English-speaking people whose ancestors came from northern Europe), and Native Americans.

When one Santa Fe woman, Carol Decker, visited Bukhara, she was struck by the fact that both cities are home to so many different types of people. "As I observed the fascinating diversity of people in the streets of Bukhara, I thought of our own multicultural Santa Fe," she said. "I wondered what we could learn from each other—if we listened."

Amy Bunting visited Bukhara in 1989 and 1991. On her first visit, she discovered the marketplace, or bazaar. "It is difficult to describe a place that both assaults and delights all the senses!" she said. Shopping in the noisy, colorful bazaar is one of the ancient traditions still followed in the old section of Bukhara. Bunting purchased many yards of beautiful rainbow-colored silk fabrics at the bazaar.

On her second visit, Bunting visited the classroom of a teacher she had met two years earlier, Musalam Satrova. Satrova taught English in a school that specialized in English-language instruction. Her students had a surprise that morning: They met an orca whale and heard whales singing! In Santa Fe, Bunting teaches classes about whales, and she took her whale presentation to Bukhara. "I gave the classes a tape of whale songs, which fascinated them," she said. As for that orca—it was a puppet.

Many Santa Fe and Bukhara students have visited one another's cities. In the summer of 1989, 12 high school students from Santa Fe spent three weeks living with

Amy Bunting's orca puppet delighted children in Bukhara.

host families in Bukhara and learning about ethnic diversity in their sister city. The students discovered that their host families were of mixed ethnic backgrounds—like many families in Santa Fe.

The students were sometimes puzzled by cultural differences. One student, Heather Black, felt smothered by her host family. They offered her food constantly (the Bukharans' way of being polite). Not wanting to offend her hosts, Heather had to start stuffing the food under her bed. Other students warmed to the attention. Mercedes Sanchez liked "the huge amount of affection in the families. It was so wonderful."

Santa Fe is home to many ethnic groups. This church reflects the city's Spanish—and Catholic—heritage.

Mercedes and another student, Laura Moffitt, wrote about their experiences in the *Albuquerque Journal North* newspaper. "The Soviets are people just like us and not our enemies," they concluded. "People of both countries share the dream of peace.... It will take trust and friendship between our countries to make this dream a reality."

Another student on the trip was Sheldon Nuñez, an Apache (uh PA chee) Indian. He said that the experience helped him grow. "My perspective of the world and my life has changed," he said. He realized that "we didn't need the finest lifestyle, but the loving support of our families and religion to survive."

This madrasa, or place of worship, in Bukhara reflects the culture of the city's Islamic people.

This girl from Bukhara got a helping hand at Las Golondrinas Ranch near Santa Fe. The historic ranch is a museum showing how early Spanish settlers lived.

Sheldon was popular with Bukharans in part because he is a Native American. "They expressed an interest in my tribal background," he reported. He found it difficult to explain to the Bukharans that Native American tribes each have a distinct language and culture, yet they share many cultural traditions.

Sheldon took along an album of historic and modern photos of Native Americans. Most of the photos were of his own tribe, the Jicarilla (hic ah REE ah) Apache. "They were stunned at the pueblos' adobe structures, which resembled their adobe homes," he said. Sheldon's performance of the Apache Hoop Dance caused a sensation in Bukhara, where the dance was described as "prehistoric."

The following summer, 13 teenagers from Bukhara traveled to Santa Fe. They noticed the familiar-looking

Bukharan students and their Santa Fe host families gathered together for a group photo while the Bukharan students were in Santa Fe.

adobe buildings, but they had never seen anything quite like the rodeo they attended! At the Cochiti (co chee tee) Indian pueblo, they visited families so they could learn about Cochiti traditions. While in Santa Fe, they stayed with host families and learned firsthand how American teenagers and their families live.

Santa Fe and Bukhara face some difficult challenges to their friendship. Since the breakup of the Soviet Union, the threat of war between it and the United States no longer exists, and the original reason for pairing Santa Fe and Bukhara is far less urgent.

Much more critical are the changes brought by the independence of Uzbekistan. Government officials in Bukhara struggle with an economy in turmoil and with political unrest. As a result, they have placed less emphasis on the sister city relationship.

Many citizens of Santa Fe and Bukhara hope that will change once Uzbekistan becomes politically and economically stable. They would like to continue their friendship through exchanges of students, professional people, and art forms—strengthening the sturdy bonds already formed between them.

Chapter Two

How Sister Cities Started

Most current sister city partnerships were formed after World War II (1939-1945). Several European countries had been enemies during the war, including France and Germany. After the war ended, many French and German citizens wanted to develop healing friendships. Their efforts led to the first pairing of sister cities in 1950, between the French town of **Montbeliard** (moan bay lee AR) and the German town of **Ludwigsburg** (LOOD vigs berg).

Other European communities soon followed. In 1951, some of them formed a new organization to help unify Europe. Members of the Council of European Municipalities (now called the Council of European Municipalities

Sister Cities Organizations

The organization responsible for most of the partnerships between cities in the United States and foreign cities is Sister Cities International (SCI). Sister Cities International was started in 1967 as an outgrowth of President Eisenhower's People to People program. The organization helps United States cities find partners and develop activities. It sponsors education, youth, and exchange programs. And it provides funding for special projects. Any city, county, state, or sister city committee can become a member of SCI by paying dues.

Other countries have their own organizations to promote sister cities. Sister Cities Italia of Italy, the Sister Cities Foundation of Argentina, the Chinese People's Association for Friendship with Foreign Countries, and the Federation of Canadian Municipalities are a few examples.

Other organizations also connect people worldwide. For example, Partners of the Americas pairs U.S. states with countries or regions in Latin America and the Caribbean. The partnership between Wisconsin and Nicaragua in Central America is one such program. People to People International—the organization formed by President Eisenhower in 1956—continues to foster international understanding through direct people-to-people exchanges.

and Regions, or CEMR) thought that sister cities would be one good way to achieve the goal of unification. They believed "the twinning of communities was an ideal political instrument for the construction of a people's Europe, developing awareness of their common heritage," according to recent CEMR members. Perhaps they were right. Over the past four decades, Europe has indeed become more united. Sister cities have likely contributed to that change.

The sister city movement in the United States began in 1956. That year President Dwight Eisenhower started a program called People to People. Eisenhower wanted individuals to get involved personally in international diplomacy.

"If people—by the millions—can reach out their hands in friendship and communicate directly the warmth of personal interest and respect, it will be a real beginning in the struggle for a peaceful world," he said.

Eisenhower wanted this personal involvement because he believed that in some ways individuals might achieve greater understanding than their governments. He encouraged them "to leap governments if necessary, to evade governments—to work out not one method but thousands of methods by which people can gradually learn a little more of each other."

Americans took the president's words to heart and began to form sister city agreements. Within just 10 years, more than 300 United States cities had found partners. And the number kept growing, until by the 1990s it had reached 1,000.

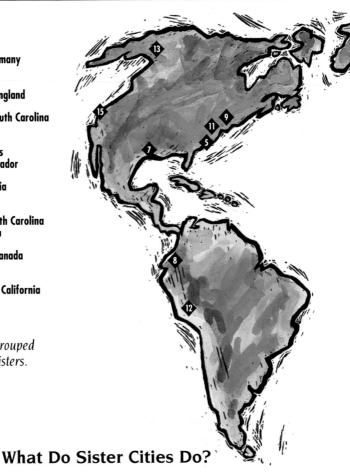

◆ 1. Frankfurt, Germany
2. Lyon, France
3. Milan, Italy
4. Birmingham, England

◆ 5. Charleston, South Carolina
6. Spoleto, Italy

◆ 7. Houston, Texas
8. Guayaquil, Ecuador

◆ 9. Reston, Virginia
10. Nyeri, Kenya

◆ 11. Charlotte, North Carolina
12. Arequipa, Peru

◆ 13. Whitehorse, Canada
14. Ushiku, Japan

◆ 15. San Francisco, California
16. Osaka, Japan
17. Taipei, Taiwan

*The cities grouped
above are sisters.*

What Do Sister Cities Do?

What sister cities do together varies as much as the cities themselves. Often they work to accomplish specific tasks such as building schools or digging ditches and wells. But sister cities get involved in many other ways as well.

Some sister cities are most interested in sharing their cultures. Sometimes they hold festivals featuring the food, art, and costumes of one or more of their sisters. For example, in 1990 the German city of **Frankfurt**

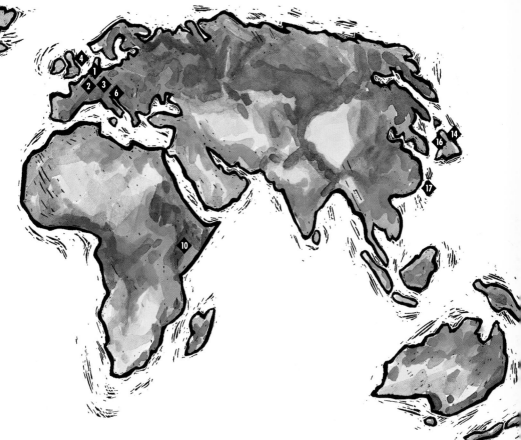

honored its nine sisters with a festival featuring music and theater performances as well as folk dances representing the many nationalities of its sister cities. The festival marked the 30th anniversary of Frankfurt's twinning with **Lyon** (lee OHN), France, and the 20th year of a four-way partnership between Frankfurt; Lyon; **Milan** (mee LAHN), Italy; and **Birmingham**, England.

The annual Spoleto (spo LEH toh) Music Festival in **Charleston**, South Carolina, is another example. It began in 1977 as a companion festival to one in **Spoleto**, Italy.

The music festival led to the sister city pairing and is the main activity of that partnership.

Other sister cities concentrate on more immediate needs. For example, maintaining a plentiful supply of clean water is a problem for many communities in developing countries. To help these communities manage their water supplies, the Council of European Municipalities and Regions (CEMR) sponsors a program called "water solidarity." With help from other international organizations, it provides money and supplies for water projects such as treatment plants and sewers.

In another type of exchange, experts share their specialized knowledge. They discuss computers, agriculture, recycling, city planning, and many other topics. For instance, firefighters from **Houston**, Texas, went to **Guayaquil** (gwi uh KEEL), Ecuador, to teach lifesaving techniques and fire prevention. They took firefighting equipment donated by a Houston company with them.

Education is another important goal. For example, **Reston**, Virginia, and **Nyeri** (nee EHR ee), Kenya, in eastern Africa, shared knowledge that will improve special education programs for mentally handicapped children in both communities.

Citizens of **Charlotte**, North Carolina, and **Arequipa** (ar ay KEE pah), Peru, cooperated to build a larger school in Arequipa. The village had hundreds of students but only one classroom. The people from Charlotte provided building supplies, and the people of Arequipa did the building. Together, they built a new school with 16 classrooms.

Neighbors Making Peace

Like Bukhara and Santa Fe, many other communities seek ways to build international understanding through sister cities. For example, the country of Israel has been in conflict for many years with its Arab neighbors. Even so, the mayor of one Israeli town hopes for an Arab sister city.

Karmiel (kar mee EL), Israel, already had a United States sister—Denver, Colorado. But when Ali Eldar, mayor of Karmiel, visited Denver, he told an audience that he hoped an Arab city would be willing to make a similar connection with Karmiel. "The great importance of sister cities is from the human standpoint. It allows people-to-people contact," he said. "People who know each other will not hate each other."

Karmiel has three other sister cities: Metz, France; Willmarsdorf (VIL mars dorf), Germany; and Kisvárda, Hungary.

Israel and its Arab neighbors have been working hard to establish better relations. For example, Israel and Jordan signed a peace treaty in 1994. A mayor's representative said that with this treaty, "It looks like Mr. Eldar's dream is beginning to take shape." Perhaps some day soon, Karmiel will find an Arab sister, and the two cities can work together for peace.

More and more, cities are joining together to promote business and trade. International trade is important because companies are able to find new markets, or
buyers, for their products. Sister city agreements often
help companies establish and develop new businesses.
The partnership between the city of **Whitehorse** in the
Yukon Territory, Canada, and **Ushiku** (oo SHEE koo),
Japan, has led to an increase in tourism between the two
cities. In addition, Ushiku stores sell gold nugget jewelry
from Whitehorse.

Some cities help their sisters by providing aid after a
disaster. After the earthquake in and around **San Francisco**, California, in 1989, two of its sister cities—**Osaka**
(oh SAH kah), Japan, and **Taipei**, Taiwan (tie PAY, tie
WAN)—gave money to help with earthquake relief.

Youth exchanges are an important part of sister city
programs. Children as young as kindergarten get involved, usually through their schools or clubs. Students
exchange letters, poetry, artwork, photos, and even
videotapes. Some students visit their sister cities to
make friends in person.

Whatever they do together, people in sister cities usually gain new insight into each other. By understanding one
another, they hope to help build a more peaceful world.

Becoming Sisters

Cities become sisters for many reasons—friendship, sharing of technical and cultural information, and the desire of citizens to help people around the world. But like the cities of Santa Fe and Bukhara, many cities are also drawn together by things they have in common. They might have the same name, similar geography or climate, or a shared cultural background.

One of the most obvious links between cities is that of having the same name. More than 50 cities in the United States are paired with foreign cities of the same name. Some of these pairings are based on name alone.

The oldest sister city pairing between a U.S. city and a foreign city—**Toledo**, Ohio, and **Toledo**, Spain—is an example. The two have been sisters for more than 60 years.

Cities with the same name often share part of their history. For example, the founders of **New Ulm**, Minnesota, named their new settlement after their former home in **Ulm**, Germany. You have probably heard of **Plymouth**, Massachusetts. Its founders, the Pilgrims, came from **Plymouth**, England. The two are now sister cities.

Carthage, Missouri, is named after the ancient city of **Carthage**, Tunisia, which is now its sister. In 1842, when the Missouri city was founded, Americans commonly named new cities after ancient ones.

Cartagena (car tuh HAY nuh), Spain, was also named after Carthage, Tunisia ("Cartagena" is the Spanish form of "Carthage"). Cartagena was founded by travelers from Carthage in 225 B.C. In turn, **Cartagena**, Colombia, in South America, was named after Cartagena, Spain. The Colombian city was founded by Spaniards and was part of their empire in the Americas until 1811. The two Cartagenas and Carthage, Tunisia, are involved in a three-way partnership.

Geography and Business

Some cities become sisters because they have similar physical features. That was the case with the two desert cities of Santa Fe, New Mexico, and Bukhara, Uzbekistan. The mountainous communities of **Sun Valley**, Idaho, and **Kitzbühel** (KITZ byoo hul), Austria, are also sisters.

Sister cities with similar geography often have similar businesses, as well. For example, both Sun Valley and Kitzbühel are ski resorts. The main business of **Lexington**, Kentucky, is the raising and racing of thoroughbred horses. Lexington's Irish sister is **County Kildare,** an entire region where horses have been raced and bred for 2,000 years. Two other sisters of Lexington are also in places where thoroughbreds are raised: **Deauville** (doh vil), France, and **Shizunai** (shih ZOO nye), Japan. "That's what connected us," said Kay Sargent, a Lexington sister city volunteer.

Cities with ports, or harbors, frequently pair up with other port cities. For example, among the sisters of **Seattle,** Washington, are **Bergen,** Norway; **Galway,** Ireland; and **Christchurch,** New Zealand. What do these cities share? They all have major shipping industries, which import and export products. Because ships from many nations visit the ports, the cities all have diverse, multiethnic populations.

History and Culture

Historical and cultural ties are very important factors in linking cities. For example, **Chicago,** Illinois, has more Polish people than any other city in the United States. What better sister for Chicago than **Warsaw,** the capital of Poland?

During the 18th and 19th centuries, Great Britain established colonies in Australia and New Zealand. The two countries remain part of the Commonwealth of Nations (those that recognize the king or queen of Great Britain as head of the country). Is it surprising that 41 Australian cities and 11 New Zealand cities are paired with British cities?

Some ties between cities are created based on name, but they develop into rich cultural exchanges. **Columbus, Ohio**, was named after Christopher Columbus, the explorer, but otherwise had no connection to him. In 1955 the city became a sister to **Genoa** (JEN oh ah), Italy, the birthplace of Christopher Columbus.

The pairing has resulted in many exchanges. For example, second graders in one class in Columbus spent

The cities grouped below are sisters.

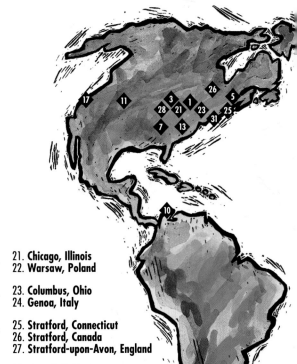

◆ 1. Toledo, Ohio
   2. Toledo, Spain

◆ 3. New Ulm, Minnesota
   4. Ulm, Germany

◆ 5. Plymouth, Massachusetts
   6. Plymouth, England

◆ 7. Carthage, Missouri
   8. Carthage, Tunisia

◆ 9. Cartagena, Spain
   10. Cartagena, Columbia

◆ 11. Sun Valley, Idaho
   12. Kitzbühel, Austria

◆ 13. Lexington, Kentucky
   14. County Kildare, Ireland
   15. Deauville, France
   16. Shizunai, Japan

◆ 17. Seattle, Washington
   18. Bergen, Norway
   19. Galway, Ireland
   20. Christchurch, New Zealand

◆ 21. Chicago, Illinois
   22. Warsaw, Poland

◆ 23. Columbus, Ohio
   24. Genoa, Italy

◆ 25. Stratford, Connecticut
   26. Stratford, Canada
   27. Stratford-upon-Avon, England

◆ 28. Council Bluffs, Iowa
   29. Tobolsk, Russia

◆ 30. Beijing, China
   31. New York City, New York

an entire school year studying Columbus. They became pen pals with a class in Genoa. The Columbus students sent a large collage of pictures they drew about life in Columbus and shared the things they learned about Christopher Columbus. In return, their Italian pen pals told them about Genoa and its history.

Three cities named Stratford have a famous playwright in common: William Shakespeare. The cities are **Stratford,**

Connecticut, in the United States; **Stratford**, Ontario, Canada; and **Stratford-upon-Avon**, England. They all hold annual festivals of plays by Shakespeare, who lived in England in the 16th century. Stratford-upon-Avon is the only city with a connection to Shakespeare: He was born there. Nevertheless, the three sisters are enriched by their associations with one another and with the great plays of Shakespeare.

How Do Cities Become Sisters?

To form a sister city partnership, most cities start with an organization or committee of people who are interested in the program. They work together to select a sister city, raise money, and decide on the types of exchanges they would like. This part of the process can take several years.

Once a city decides on a possible sister, its mayor or

This Bukharan girl smiled at Santa Fe friends waiting to meet her at the Santa Fe airport. When cities decide to become sisters, their citizens—including students—often visit each other.

other official may write an invitation. Sam Pick, the mayor of Santa Fe, New Mexico, began a letter to Bukhara, Uzbekistan, like this:

> *Dear Sirs and Madams:*
>   *I am writing to invite Bukhara to become a sister city with Santa Fe. A group of citizens of this capital city in the state of New Mexico recently had the pleasure of visiting your fine city. They were so impressed by the culture and history of Bukhara that they came to me with the idea of forming a sister city relationship.*

Most sister city agreements involve visits of citizens between the cities. When **Council Bluffs,** Iowa, wanted to establish a tie with **Tobolsk** (tuh BOLSK), Russia, groups visited back and forth "to look each other over," they said, and to plan for the future. The first goal for Council Bluffs and Tobolsk was to sign a charter, or formal agreement. Usually a charter outlines the terms of the partnership.

Once the papers are signed, the people in both cities will have to keep the partnership going. "We must make a great effort to put life into the signing of this charter," said the mayor of Tobolsk. "The final result must be person-to-person communication." Citizens may choose to get involved through trade, sharing their arts, exchanging information, or helping each other through a crisis.

If people in both of the sister cities have a genuine interest in a sister city relationship and a strong desire to learn and to make new friends, their partnership will probably be successful.

Obstacles to Sister City Partnerships

Many people view language as a serious barrier to forming sister city partnerships. This attitude is usually overcome once a partnership has been established. People discover they can communicate in many ways. Even so, countries with less well-known languages (for example, Greece and Portugal) have problems finding sisters.

Not every sister city friendship goes smoothly or lasts forever. Sometimes governments interfere. Hostilities between the governments of Cuba and the United States have prevented pairings between their cities. Likewise, national clashes have kept Pakistani cities from pairing with Indian cities and North Korean cities from pairing with those in South Korea.

The partnership between **Beijing** (bay jing) in the People's Republic of China and **New York City** in the United States is an example of how sister city ties can be affected by governments. China had no sister cities until 1979. Some of China's communist leaders didn't want its people to learn about the world beyond China's borders. In the 1970s they bowed to pressure from other countries and began to end China's isolation. With the opening of China's doors, its cities made more than 365 partnerships. New York City and Beijing, China's capital, became sisters in 1980.

In 1989, however, things changed again. Chinese students and other citizens in Beijing demonstrated in favor of democracy. The Chinese military killed hundreds of

The Great Wall of China symbolizes that country's long isolation from much of the world. But in 1979, China began to open its doors to sister city relationships.

the protestors. After the demonstration, many people were arrested. Some were executed. These harsh actions angered many other nations. In protest, New York City suspended its partnership with Beijing.

Sister city relationships can be difficult to maintain amid political change. As the countries that were once part of the Soviet Union struggle to build their governments and economies, they are often unable to keep up the sister city ties they formed during their years as Soviet states.

Finally, political and ethical values can be an obstacle for sister cities. For example, many people in the world condemned the official policy of apartheid (the separation of racial groups) that existed for many years in South Africa. As a result, very few cities chose South African sisters. With apartheid officially ended in South Africa, South African cities may begin to form bonds with other cities.

Chapter Four

Learning without Boundaries

People don't need to know a foreign language to experience the beauty of a song or a design. They don't need to know all the facts about a country to enjoy the shapes of its buildings or the colors of its national costume. So art forms are another road to understanding—a kind of learning without boundaries.

Nearly all sister city programs involve the arts—dance, music, painting, sculpture, architecture, poetry, and other forms of expression. School choirs, folk dance groups, and art exhibits travel across borders and oceans as sister cities share the best of their cultures.

Young artists of all kinds have many opportunities to participate in sister cities art projects. Many involve the exchange of drawings and murals. Young people often perform dances, songs, and plays for visitors from their sister cities. When they are learning about foreign cultures, they make traditional costumes and learn art forms of other countries.

Each year Sister Cities International (SCI) sponsors a competition for artists between the ages of 13 and 18. The contest allows young artists to express themselves in support of the goals of sister cities programs. Competition begins on a local level. Winners of local contests can then enter the SCI competition.

The Arts of Japan

The Japanese are well known for their meditation gardens. The gardens are places for rest and reflection. Usually they are carefully groomed—gardeners rake the gravel paths and borders into neat patterns and pick up every fallen leaf. Still ponds and artfully trimmed shrubs and trees give the gardens a subtle beauty.

One Japanese city wanted its sister city in the United States to enjoy a meditation garden. Citizens of **Awata** (ah WAH tah), Japan, sent a plan for one to their sister, **Mountain View**, California. They also sent materials— including five huge boulders.

The people of Mountain View followed the plan, arranging the boulders according to the drawings from Awata. The five boulders are surrounded by white gravel raked in neat rows, Japanese style. The garden is called Tenryu No Aoishi (ten-REE-oo noh ah-oh-EE-shee), which means "Blue Rocks from the River Tenryu." As citizens of Mountain View visit the "Blue Rocks from the River Tenryu"—rocks plucked from a river thousands of miles away—perhaps they are thinking of the kindness, and ingenuity, of their Japanese friends.

Another gift from a Japanese sister shows what a Japanese home is like. A Japanese townhouse that is now in **Boston,** Massachusetts, was a gift from Boston's sister city, **Kyoto** (kee OH toh), Japan. The 100-year-old structure was once a shop and home in the silk-weaving district of Kyoto. It has been fitted with plumbing, furniture, and a garden to show how a Japanese family might live today.

This Kyoto townhouse in Boston teaches the people of that city about the rich culture of Japan.

The townhouse is the focal point of the Japan Program offered by Boston's Children's Museum. The house is called Kyō no machiya (kee-OH no mah-CHEE-ah), which means "Kyoto-style townhouse and shop." Money for the house was raised by both Kyoto and the Boston Sister City Fund. The house was brought to Boston in parts and reconstructed in 1980 by craftsmen from Kyoto.

Since the house was installed, the connection between Kyoto and the Children's Museum has grown. Museum staff members visit Japan every year to seek new information for the program. In turn, Kyoto officials visit the museum to offer expert advice. The results: rich friendships and an authentic cultural program about Japanese society.

Student Exchanges

Exchanges of students are perhaps the most popular type of sister city exchange. International students visit their sister cities in the United States (some even live with host families for a year or more). In turn, young people from the United States also visit and study abroad.

Students who participate in exchanges learn about geography, government, international relations, and foreign languages. They learn to participate in and organize group activities. Best of all, they learn to make friends with many kinds of people.

An exchange between another Japanese city and one in the United States shows how much students can learn from each other. **Kameoka** (kah mee OH kah), Japan, and

In Kameoka, Stillwater students tasted the waters of Kiyomizu Temple, which means "pure water temple."

Stillwater, Oklahoma, have been sister cities since 1984. During the same time, the state of Oklahoma and Kyoto Prefecture, where Kameoka is located, have been sister states. In addition, Stillwater Middle School is a sister school to Taisei (ty say) Junior High of Kameoka.

In 1990, 12 students and 7 adults from Taisei Junior High visited Stillwater for four days. They stayed with host families and visited their sister school.

Then, later in the year, 12 Stillwater students visited Kameoka for a week. Mostly they spent time with Japanese host families, but they also visited their sister school. They kept journals during the trip. When they returned

When students from Stillwater Middle School visited students at Taisei Junior High in Kameoka, they played a game to get acquainted.

A view of Kameoka

to Stillwater, they told the *Stillwater NewsPress* about Japanese people, family life, and schools.

One of them noticed a difference in the way adults and youth interacted in Kameoka. "The families communicated with each other better than in the United States," said Terrence Anderson. "The kids obeyed their parents all the time."

But Christian Szlichta had a slightly different impression. "I thought Japanese students would be very quiet and hard-working. Boy, I was wrong. They threw paper airplanes and played baseball in the halls. They talked whenever they wanted during class."

Stillwater Middle School students who didn't go to

Kameoka get a chance to learn about their sister city when their school holds Kameoka Week every year. During a recent Kameoka Week, one class learned the precise folds of origami (the Japanese craft of creating fanciful shapes out of paper). Down the hall, another class studied haiku poetry. Other students enjoyed a Japanese tea ceremony and saw a traditional Kabuki puppet theater performance.

In addition, throughout each day, students made announcements over the school's P.A. system:

"Kameoka is located about 15 miles from Kyoto, one of Japan's largest cities."

"Kameoka's old name was Kameyama."

"Kameoka's population is nearly 90,000."

Stillwater Middle School also includes Japanese topics in school activities and classes throughout the year. And most students at the school have pen pals at Taisei Junior High. Kameoka Week is just one of the activities that enrich the partnership between Stillwater Middle School and Taisei Junior High. Learning about a sister city is even more rewarding when you take an active role in sharing knowledge and experiences.

Going to School in the United States

Occasionally a sister city agreement can lead to a student spending an entire school year—or longer—in a sister city. One such student is Andrey, a young man from the city of Dushanbe, Tadzhikistan (doo SHAM beh, tah jeek uh STAN). Tadzhikistan, once part of the Soviet

Union, is located in central Asia. It is now an independent republic.

Andrey's family and a family in Boulder, Colorado, became friends in 1989. They heard about each other when Kelly, a son in the Boulder family, stayed with Andrey's family in Dushanbe. **Dushanbe** and **Boulder** are sister cities. Kelly was a member of the first Boulder-Dushanbe high school exchange group.

The next year, Andrey visited Boulder with a group of students from Dushanbe. He stayed with his Boulder family. "We grew very fond of him and invited him to come back," said Miriam, Andrey's American "mother."

Andrey joined their family in January 1991. He was in the ninth grade then, and he planned to complete his entire high school education at Boulder High School. "I wanted to improve my English," he explained.

He planned to graduate in 1994. But in 1991, he was faced with the prospect of staying longer in Boulder. Unstable conditions in Tadzhikistan made it dangerous for him to go home. Civil wars between Muslim rebels and the Russia-backed Tadzhikistan military caused the country's economy and social structure to collapse.

Andrey's parents lost their jobs and are living on money they had saved. They would like to leave Dushanbe, but so far, they have not been able to do so. Andrey is very worried. "My father said, 'Don't even think about coming back,'" he said. Andrey's sister is also living in Boulder. "My parents are really happy that both of their children are in a safe place," said Andrey. To protect his parents, Andrey has requested that his family

Civil war rocked Tadzhikistan during the early
1990s. Here, soldiers patrol the streets of
Dushanbe, Andrey's hometown. As a result of
the political upheaval, Andrey's stay in the
United States has been extended. Andrey may
become a permanent exile.

Andrey, *far right*, has found a loving second family in Boulder.

name and the name of his Boulder family not be printed in this book.

Andrey graduated in 1995 and is attending a local community college.

Andrey explained that schools in his country are more difficult than schools in the United States. "There is a choice [of subjects] in the United States. The program in the Tadzhik schools consists of 15 subjects, and each student does all of them. We go to school six days a week from eight o'clock to two o'clock. Each class is 45 minutes long, and we do not have a lunch break." To attend classes in all 15 subjects, he explained, the students have different schedules on different days.

During his time off from classes in Boulder, Andrey likes to go camping with his Boulder family and friends. He thinks kids in the United States are friendly, "but I have to speak first." When he started playing football, he discovered that his popularity went up a lot. Before he came to the United States, he thought that Americans had few problems. "Now I know that the United States has problems, too," he said. Two of them, he said, are high taxes and the condition of roads.

Andrey is excited about being in the United States. Only a few years ago, he said, "an exchange like this was impossible." The move toward democracy among the republics of the former Soviet Union made Andrey's visit to Boulder possible. Since antidemocracy forces have once again taken over in his own country, Andrey may become a permanent exile from his home.

Chapter Five

For Love of Earth

One of the most critical problems facing people in many parts of the world is a shortage of food. Many people worry that humans are using more resources than the earth can supply. They are afraid that more and more people will starve if we don't come up with more efficient ways to grow crops and distribute food.

Some sister cities are working together to improve agricultural methods—ways to grow more and better crops. For example, from 1988 to 1992, a remote California farming region worked with two tiny towns in Costa Rica to develop farming methods that were both productive and safe for the environment.

People in the farm country of **Anderson Valley** in northern California helped farmers in **Guayabo** (gwy AH

California's lush farmland gave Costa Rican farmers new ideas for growing their own crops.

bo) and **La Fortuna** (LA for TOON ah), Costa Rica, learn to grow products for themselves and for export while maintaining the beauty of their land.

As part of this plan, Costa Rican students studied production, marketing, and farming techniques at the Anderson Valley Agricultural Institute. On returning home, they shared their new knowledge and skills with other Costa Rican farmers.

One Costa Rican farmer, Juan Carlos Calvo, studied in Anderson Valley from 1991 to 1992. He planned to teach other farmers about organic farming when he returned home. "People use too many chemicals," he said, "and we want to change that." His experiences at the Agricultural Institute helped him appreciate Costa Rica. "It helps me see what a beautiful country we have," he said.

Reaching Self-Sufficiency: Esabalu and Amesbury

Townspeople in **Amesbury,** Massachusetts, are helping villagers in **Esabalu** (es ah BAH loo), Kenya, in eastern Africa learn sustainable farming methods (ways to farm that do not hurt the land).

The program focuses on exchanges of skills and ideas rather than money and technology, said Dr. Mark Bean. He is the chairman of Amesbury for Africa, the sister city organization in Amesbury. "Our assistance is a helping hand," he explained, "not a handout."

The sister city agreement began in 1987, when Amesbury for Africa joined forces with the Esabalu Self Help Group, an organization of about 100 local families. The two groups began looking for

This Esabalu farmer is wearing a cap that reads "Amesbury."

ways to promote self-sufficiency in the village—that is, ways that the villagers could help themselves.

The Esabalu Self Help Group applies for grant money and arranges for training in new approaches and techniques. Each year, experts from Amesbury travel to Esabalu to help in four general areas: food production, income generation, health, and education.

One food production project, a maize (corn) growing program, was not completely successful. The plan involved distribution of special seed and training in new growing methods. It had two goals: to allow the villagers to grow enough maize to sell some, but also to keep some for their own use.

When they began to grow the maize, however, farmers found they could not depend on a good crop. They did not get enough rain, and their growing plots were too small, among other factors. They discovered they couldn't earn enough money selling maize to purchase next year's seeds and fertilizer.

To solve these problems, members of the Esabalu Self Help Group looked for ways the farmers could earn money from other agricultural projects. Several plans have emerged from their efforts. One plan is market gardening—growing crops to sell but not to use themselves.

So far, beekeeping is the most successful of these projects. Bill Ongute, Esabalu's chief beekeeper, describes it as "a good enterprise." His five hives produce about 65 bottles of honey every three months and bring in an income higher than a teacher's. Esabalu farmers are also considering raising pigs, poultry, and rabbits for profit.

Another problem facing the Esabalu villagers is a constant shortage of water. Said Ongute, "Agriculture cannot

Esabalu farmers have produced record yields in recent years.

succeed as a business enterprise" without a dependable supply of water. Esabalu needs to develop a dependable one. The Esabalu Self Help Group is exploring a well-drilling project with help from international organizations and from Amesbury for Africa.

Despite problems, Esabalu has been producing eight times more food since the exchange began. In addition, Esabalu villagers have learned to plan and manage long-term projects that benefit their village.

Replanting Trees:
Oaxaca and Palo Alto

Palo Alto, California, and **Oaxaca** (wah HAH ca), Mexico, have been sisters for 30 years. They have cooperated on many projects. For example, in 1976 they built a

Majestic hills surround the Mexican city of Oaxaca.

The people of Oaxaca and Palo Alto are replanting sites such as this one with ocote pine.

planetarium and observatory in Oaxaca. In 1989, the two communities began a project to benefit the ecology of the Oaxaca valley.

The first stage of the project is reforestation in the valley. Many trees on the hills of the area have been cut down. Trees are not able to grow back as quickly as people cut them down. As a result, the hills near Oaxaca are becoming bare.

The people of Oaxaca would like to see their hillsides covered with trees again. In particular, they would like to see thick forests of ocote (oh COAT eh) pine, a native tree. Many citizens of Palo Alto—a community with many trees—also have a great desire to see their sister city surrounded by trees. The partnership between the two cities is helping the Oaxacans replant their forests.

The project involves planting new trees. But it also includes a new way to irrigate the trees, explained Joyce Leonard, a member of Palo Alto Neighbors Abroad. "Palo Alto introduced the concept of drip irrigation to Oaxaca," she said. Drip irrigation is a method of watering plants on a schedule. A California company, Rainbird Corporation, donated an irrigation system and sent an expert to teach Oaxacans about the system and about the importance of irrigation. Citizens in Palo Alto are working to raise funds for construction tools and irrigation equipment. The people of Oaxaca are doing the digging and planting.

The first trees were planted in spring 1990. Planting trees in Oaxaca is a difficult job because the soil is rocky.

In addition, the seedlings must be irrigated for two years to give them a good start. Trees not reached by the irrigation system must be watered by hand.

Keeping the project going can be a struggle. Leonard admitted, "It isn't all instant success." Many of the first trees were killed by drought before the irrigation system was in place. Some trees were killed by vandalism. Then some surviving trees were trampled by people who were unaware of the project.

"These first trees must be successful if the project is going to work," explained Leonard. Otherwise, the project may lose people's support. Teaching people about the importance of the reforestation project may help prevent vandalism and accidental trampling.

Once established, the new trees will help prevent erosion in Oaxaca's hills, help keep the air clean, provide habitat for birds and animals, and add to Oaxaca's natural beauty. No matter where a tree is planted, said Leonard, "it benefits the world."

Sister Cities and the Environment: Louisville and Quito

Many sister city programs are working to help solve environmental problems. Citizens of **Louisville,** Kentucky, and **Quito** (KEE toh), Ecuador, are concerned about clean water and waste management. In 1990, Quito's mayor, Rodrigo Paz Delgado, won an award from the United Nations for his efforts to clean up his city's environment. People in Louisville saw his program as a chance to strengthen their ties with their sister in South America.

The two cities, sisters since 1962, are similar in some ways. Both have populations of about one million people. Both are surrounded by farmland.

In addition, Quito faces a problem Louisville faced about 30 years ago. The city is growing rapidly, expanding beyond its ability to manage its waste. With its supermodern, high-tech system of waste disposal, Louisville is in a good position to share some of what it has learned about planning and managing a large sewage system.

The two cities are cooperating to help solve the problem of three kinds of waste: industrial wastewater, hazardous materials, and solid waste. Industrial wastewater is water that has been used by industry. It must be specially treated before being discharged into sewers, and then treated again before going into a river. Hazardous materials include both solid and liquid wastes that are poisonous. They must be disposed of carefully so they don't hurt people or animals or contaminate surrounding land. Solid waste is what you recycle, compost, or put in your trash can. It, too, needs to be disposed of safely.

In Quito, industries had not been required by law to pretreat wastewater or control the sewage they dumped into the public sewer system. Quito officials wanted to change that. They traveled to the United States to observe Louisville's approach, and they continue to work with experts from Louisville to change this situation.

Visitors study the Witten exhibit.

Environment in Danger

Some projects involve simply making people aware of problems. In 1987, for instance, Witten (VITT en), Germany, and its four sister cities created an exhibit focused on environmental problems. Part of the exhibit, "Environment in Danger," focused on the causes and effects of pollution. Another part featured paintings by artists from the participating cities.

The exhibit traveled to each of the sister cities, which are located in France, Great Britain, Germany, and Israel. According to Witten officials, the exhibit was "an excellent way to better unite the partner cities."

The city of Quito is concerned about environmental problems.

In turn, Louisville engineers have visited Quito to observe that city's sewer construction and landfill programs. (A landfill is a large hole or mound where solid waste is deposited. Eventually, the hole or mound is covered with dirt.) While in Quito, the engineers also advised Quito engineers about ways to manage and expand their sewage and waste systems. Louisville is also sharing its computer programs for the design of drainage systems.

This cooperative effort has led to other exchanges. For example, the Louisville wastewater agency sent used computers to 20 schools in Quito in 1994. Soon Quito students will communicate by e-mail with Louisville students. They will explore environmental projects together as they learn about computers, foreign language, and their sister city friends.

Because of the Louisville-Quito program, many citizens are realizing that environmental problems are universal. "We must learn to solve our problems together," said Quito's Mayor Paz Delgado, "or we will fail in our responsibility for future generations to come."

Chapter Six

Friends Mean Business

Many companies want to buy and sell products around the world. Most companies are located in or near cities, so one way to accomplish this kind of trade is with sister city agreements. In fact, cities often choose their sisters with trade in mind. In other cases, a successful trade partnership grows out of a sister city agreement. However it happens, cities are finding that their sisters can often provide opportunities for doing business.

One example is the trade partnership between the Chinese city of **Xiamen** (shyah mun) and the U.S. city of **Baltimore,** Maryland. A Baltimore company sells engines in China. Chinese companies use the engines to make

The port city of Portland, *above*, trades millions of dollars worth of products with its sister, Sapporo.

construction equipment. The construction equipment is then sold to the United States and other countries. The partnership benefits both sisters.

Eastern European countries are seeking the benefits of trade as well. Since 1989, many countries there have formed new governments. Formerly they had been under communist rule. The new governments (unlike many of the former governments) allow trade and other types of contact with the rest of the world.

One type of new contact may be sister city relationships. People in eastern European cities are hungry for modern products and ways of doing business. In turn, some of them make products they would like to sell outside their own borders. Having sister cities can help, and city officials are eager to form partnerships.

Portland, Oregon, and **Sapporo**, Japan, have been active sisters since 1959. They trade several hundred million dollars worth of products each year. The trade has focused on the export of Oregon wood chips and grass seed to Hokkaido (ho KYE doh) Prefecture, the island state in which Sapporo is located. The success of this partnership has led to the export of other Portland products, including coffee and clam chowder.

The trade partnership grew out of the sister city partnership. Linda Fromm, who is a member of the Portland-Sapporo Sister City Association, explained, "The trade relationship is a result of the close ties formed during the cultural exchanges over the years."

Adding business deals to the partnership has not always been easy. The partners must find the right products for export and import, and they must generate support in the community. "Until you develop relationships and understanding with one another, trade is difficult," said Fromm.

Sapporo's city officials are dedicated to the trade aspect of the sister city relationship. "They take it very seriously," according to Fromm. Until recently, Portland officials focused on cultural rather than economic exchanges. That may change, Fromm predicts, as more people in Portland see the benefits of trading with their sister.

Another U.S. city is exporting computer technology. San Jose (san hoh ZAY), California, is in the center of what is known as Silicon Valley, an area with many technology-oriented companies. For example, Intel Corporation, the huge maker of computer chips, is located in the valley. Through its Office of Economic Development, San Jose is working to increase foreign sales of products from Silicon Valley companies. The office also hopes to create jobs in the San Jose area and to make the city more visible in the world's markets.

San Jose and **Dublin**, Ireland, have been sisters since 1986. Intel Corporation established a large office in Dublin in 1991. Another 25 Silicon Valley companies have opened branch offices in Dublin, helping to make Dublin an important center for high techology in Europe. Also, many students from Ireland have spent summers in Silicon Valley, working as interns in the valley's high-tech companies.

Another chance for sharing information comes during San Jose's Irish Week each March. Irish businesspeople choose that week to visit San Jose—sometimes accompanied by the Lord Mayor of Dublin. They celebrate Saint Patrick's Day with their sister city, and then they get down to business by meeting with Silicon Valley executives. These business forums give both groups a chance to explore future exchanges.

Other California cities also have Irish sisters—**San Francisco** is paired with **Cork**, and **Los Gatos** is a sister to **Listowel**. In 1993, Silicon Valley's Seagate Technology, the world's largest maker of computer disk drives, built a large factory in Londonderry in Northern Ireland. And an unofficial economic partnership has developed between all of Ireland (both Northern Ireland and the Republic of Ireland) and the region of northern California.

Sister Cities and Technical Exchanges

Some cities share knowledge about technology, science, or city government. Rochester, New York, is helping its sisters develop medical knowledge. At the same time, Rochester students get a chance to work abroad.

The idea started with assistance to sister city **Bamako, Mali** (bah MAH koh, MAH lee), in Africa. The people of **Rochester** have sent medical supplies to clinics in Bamako and have trained health workers there. The city of **Rennes** (REN), France, helps Rochester transport supplies to Bamako. This program ties cities on three different continents together.

Fort Worth, Texas, is exchanging information with its sisters about independent living for people who use wheelchairs. At the same time, the city has had a chance to cheer as wheelchair basketball teams compete. Wheelchair basketball teams from both Italy and Japan have challenged the team of the University of Texas at Arlington (known as the Wheelchair Mavericks). One team, which visited in 1989, was from **Reggio Emilia,** Italy. A team from **Nagaoka** (na ga OH ka), Japan, came in 1991. Both teams gained new friends in their sister city. They visited during Fort Worth's Sister Cities Week, held every year in September. They joined Fort Worth's disabled citizens in meetings, discussions, and other activities focused on topics of concern to disabled people.

The city of **Greenville**, South Carolina, asked its sister, **Bergamo** (BEAR gah moh), Italy, for expert help with an urban problem. Greenville needed a new attraction to draw people downtown. Greenville's own attempt to create an attractive downtown area—the Coffee Street Mall—had failed to become a center of activity.

In 1986, when some Greenville citizens visited their new

sister city in northern Italy, they knew they had the answer. Bergamo's beautiful piazzas, or public squares, are bustling centers of activity. Could Greenville capture that atmosphere for itself? In particular, could Greenville transform its empty Coffee Street Mall into a busy Italian piazza?

A piazza in Bergamo

The idea appealed to Greenville city leaders. They thought it might help revive Greenville's city center and improve the city's economy. The project might also reinforce the bond between Bergamo and Greenville. The new public square could be named Piazza Bergamo. It would keep that city in the minds of Greenville citizens.

For the next three years, the two cities cooperated in a project to create an Italian piazza in Greenville. An architect from Bergamo, Laura Sonzogni, volunteered to spend

The new public square designed for Greenville is named Piazza Bergamo after Greenville's Italian sister.

her vacation one summer in Greenville working on a design. When she presented her plan to the city, she explained that the piazza is the center of social activity in Italian cities. "The square is a place of common property," she said. To bring citizens downtown, she said, Greenville needed "something really special, something you can't find anywhere else."

The key to Laura Sonzogni's design was simplicity. "The

Italian squares have large empty spaces with one element like a fountain or a sculpture in the center," she explained. "Nothing else disturbs the view." The main elements of her design included a covered patio, an amphitheater, an Italian-style fountain, and an arched gateway.

The design was on view for several months so that everyone in Greenville would have a chance to comment on it. After making a few changes, city officials accepted the design and began construction.

The piazza was finally ready to open in October 1989. Bergamo officials traveled to Greenville for the opening ceremonies. Antonello Pezzini, head of the Bergamo delegation, said, "This brings together the friendship of two cities." The opening of Piazza Bergamo was celebrated in Bergamo as well, with a full report in the local newspaper.

The piazza project is considered a success. It brought together many segments of Greenville. It strengthened the ties between Bergamo and Greenville. And it set the stage for future activities, including business and technical exchanges.

Chapter Seven

Reaching Out to a Friend

eople's desire to help others is an important factor in many sister pairings. This impulse to reach out is called humanitarianism. Usually people make humanitarian gestures without expecting something in return. For instance, **Lucca** (LOO kah), an Italian city, organized a joint effort with its four sister cities to help a town in Bolivia (in South America) build a water-treatment plant and increase the amount of clean drinking water.

Sometimes the aid is returned. **San Jose,** California, and **San Jose,** Costa Rica, are both in areas where earthquakes occur. Ties between them began in 1965, when Costa Rica suffered an earthquake. San Jose, its capital city, was badly damaged. The citizens of the California city sent equipment and crews to help clean up the Costa Rican city.

Years later, the Costa Ricans were able to return the favor. An earthquake in 1989 hit San Jose, California, and other cities in the San Francisco Bay Area. The Costa Ricans responded generously by sending urgently needed supplies.

A humanitarian act may lead to other types of exchanges. The partnership between Yamanashi Prefecture in Japan and the state of Iowa is a busy, prosperous one—but it began with a disaster. The cities of **Kōfu** in Yamanashi and **Des Moines,** the capital of Iowa, became sisters in 1958. Then, in 1959, Yamanashi was hit by a typhoon. The typhoon destroyed the countryside and started a severe flood.

The state of Iowa quickly sent aid, especially hogs and grain to feed the people of Yamanashi. The aid soon turned to trade. Iowa farmers now export hogs and feed, along with other farm animals and products, to Yamanashi Prefecture and other parts of Japan. These two regions were able to turn an unexpected crisis into a lasting friendship.

A Garbage Truck Powered by Friendship: Ann Arbor and Juigalpa

The sister city partnership between **Ann Arbor,** Michigan, and **Juigalpa** (wee GAL pah), Nicaragua, is based on the desire of people in Ann Arbor to help their friends in Juigalpa. In 1986, the people of Nicaragua had been

The road to Juigalpa was a long one for three men from Ann Arbor. They chose to drive from home to their sister city in Nicaragua with a special gift—a garbage truck.

engaged in a civil war for seven years. The war was costing many lives and using up money and resources. Many people in the country were (and still are) very poor. Children went without shoes and often without food.

Ann Arbor and Juigalpa became *ciudades hermanas* (sister cities) in 1986. A group of Ann Arbor citizens visited

Juigalpa at the end of that year. They wrote a report that said, "Residents of our sister city have no sewage system, an uncertain water supply, limited health-care resources, and an economy that barely meets the basic needs of most citizens. Despite these difficult conditions, our hosts were optimistic, energetic, warmhearted, and willing to share their homes and lives with us."

The Ann Arbor delegation wanted to show an equal openheartedness. "We asked them to suggest what we could do to help solve one of the community's most pressing problems," said Kurt Berggren, one of the Ann Arbor group. What did the Juigalpans suggest? They had problems getting their garbage away from their homes to a dump, since they had no garbage truck. They wanted a truck.

The Ann Arbor citizens returned home determined to buy one. In about half a year, they raised over $22,000—the cost of a Haul-All Model 12. This small, sturdy truck would be able to travel the narrow, winding roads in the hills of Juigalpa. On the doors of *el camion blanco* ("the white truck") they printed the words "Juigalpa-Ann Arbor Ciudades Hermanas."

The next problem was getting the truck to Juigalpa. Because the cost of shipping the truck was so great, three men—Kurt Berggren, Kip Eckroad, and Tom Rieke—decided to drive it the 4,300 miles to Juigalpa. They saved money by driving, but the men also liked the "personal touch of actually delivering it," said Berggren.

The drive took two and a half weeks—weeks that turned out to be full of adventure. The Ann Arbor men had trouble crossing the border into Mexico because they didn't have the correct papers. They drove in nearly constant rainfall. One man had to ride in the back of the truck (the place where the garbage goes), and he was usually soaking wet because of the open top. When they drove through the country of Honduras (own DUR ahs), the men were stopped by armed police every 30 or 40

Scooting down a canyon toward Juigalpa is the Haul-All Model 12 from Ann Arbor.

miles. Each time, the police inspected the entire truck and everything in it.

At last, as Rieke put it, "Three bedraggled Ann Arborites arrived in Juigalpa. The truck was filthy but otherwise in perfect condition." A curious, happy crowd greeted the adventurers. After the truck was washed, the three Americans covered it with banners and letters bearing goodwill messages from Ann Arbor.

Rito Siles Blanco, the mayor of Juigalpa, was overwhelmed with the way the truck was delivered—in person. He promised to tell the story in Juigalpa's schools "as an example of people caring for each other."

To most Juigalpans, the garbage truck was a welcome gift. It was put to work immediately, making its rounds every day of the year. Clearly the truck was needed. According to Mayor Siles, "It's helped us clean up the center

After a good washing, Juigalpa's garbage truck was festooned with banners, *above opposite*. *Below opposite*, crowds gathered to congratulate the truck's drivers, *right*.

marketplace and better service the hospital. It helps the entire community."

Some other citizens of Juigalpa were not as happy about the truck. It is such a small solution to a very big problem, they said. Also, the truck often needs new parts. When it broke down in the winter of 1989–1990, almost a year passed before people in Ann Arbor were able to send all the necessary parts to make the truck run again. Juigalpans have the skills to fix the truck, but getting parts will always be a problem.

Still, "one garbage truck can make a difference," said Joaquin Gomez of the Nicaraguan Embassy in Washington. In his view, a garbage truck can be an important step in solving the problems of disease and poor sanitation. Together, people can overcome their daily problems—even big ones—step by step, truck by truck.

Chapter Eight

Sister Cities and You

Is there a place for young people—for you—in sister cities programs? The answer is yes! You can't drive a garbage truck to Nicaragua (at least, not yet), but you can participate in sister city programs. Each year thousands of young people do. All you need is a desire to learn and to be a friend.

Andrey, the Tadzhik student attending school in Boulder, Colorado, advises young people to get to know international students in their communities. They can also try to become exchange students themselves. "Exchange students can share information with each other's families, who then share the information with more friends. Then they don't have to be afraid of each other any more," said Andrey. Students can embark on "a mission of peace on the planet through exchange programs."

Make a Visit

Sometimes students from the United States are able to travel abroad to their sister cities. The experience was invaluable for Erica Southworth, a student at the University of North Carolina at Chapel Hill. She traveled extensively and met other students around the world through the youth program of Sister Cities of Raleigh, North Carolina. Here she is pictured in Paris. When Erica later heard about bombings in Israel and war in Yugoslavia (you go SLAHV ee ah), they had a personal meaning to her because she had made friends in both places.

Exchange students such as Erica often share their experiences with classmates when they return home. By inviting exchange students to talk about their travels, other students can "travel" with them.

But you don't need to travel abroad to be a "world citizen." Young people around the world learn about one another through many kinds of activities. For example, school children often serve as a kind of welcoming committee to sister city visitors. In **Eugene**, Oregon, middle school students made friendship bracelets for visiting students from **Irkutsk** (er KOTSK), Siberia.

How Do You Get Involved?

If you want to get involved with sister cities, first find out if your city has any sisters. Your teacher or librarian might be able to help you. You could call the city government offices to find out. If you're not sure which office to call, try the office of the mayor.

You could also call or write to Sister Cities International. If you do live in a sister city, SCI can tell you about your city's program. It might offer activities specifically for youth, as many sister cities do. SCI's address and phone number are listed at the end of this book.

Even if your city does not have a sister, you can join in (or help organize) activities that will connect you to young people in other countries. Try some of the following ideas.

Find a Pen Pal

It's fun and interesting—and challenging!—to write letters to foreign students. Writing is an excellent way to get to know someone in a different culture, and many youth have pen pals in their sister cities. For example, in **Champaign** (sham PAIN), Illinois, students write to pen pals in **Tartu** (tar TOO), a large city in the eastern part of Estonia. The Tartu students write back in English, telling about their families, pets, and school. Several organizations can help you find a pen pal. Check the list at the end of this book.

Once you've found a pen pal, how will you communicate? If you don't speak the same language, you can draw pictures. Why not take photographs of yourself and your friends doing things you enjoy?

Some students send videotapes to each other. Fourth and fifth graders from Loretto Elementary School in **Jacksonville,** Florida, made a videotape for their sister school in **Murmansk,** Russia. In the video, the students tell about their school and city. After taking viewers on a video tour of the school, they show after-school activities and sports, explain American holidays, and describe family life.

The video was produced by Jane Fleetwood of Continental Cablevision. In making the tape, she said, "The students used their ideas and their words. They really felt like they were making a connection with kids on the other side of the world."

Messages that require high-tech equipment can be a problem, however. The Jacksonville students discovered that VCRs are not very common in Murmansk. Fewer students in Murmansk were able to see the video than they had hoped. Even so, the Jacksonville students have made the first step in reaching out to people in another culture.

If your pen pals own video equipment, and if your school has a video camera, you could film events at your school. If this equipment is not available, you could send a class banner with friendship messages in English, your sister city's language, or many different languages. Make a bulletin board and take pictures of it to send. Or collect a box of artwork to share.

Your pen pals would probably also enjoy an audio tape of your favorite music. (Remember to consider whether tape recorders are available in your pen pals' communities.)

You could even send a party. Some students in Champaign sent party supplies to a school in their sister city,

My name is Silver Iraat. I'm nine. I am in form three. I live in Tartu. Tartu is not a big town, but here is a university. I think, that Tartu is a beautiful town. I have mother, father, and one sister. My mother's name is Aili. My father's name is Ullo. My sister's name is Siiri. I have a cat. His's name is Nuki.

A Tartu student sent this letter to a pen pal in Champaign.

The artist of this SCI greeting card, Kim Cammack, 17, of Tempe, Arizona, envisions the world as a mixing bowl with a recipe for peace.

Tartu. They wanted to share a long-distance party, so they collected and wrapped candy, colored pencils, videotapes, and other gifts.

Remember, with anything you send, you can include messages of peace and friendship. In 1989, fourth and fifth graders in **Norfolk,** Virginia, competed in a contest to write a poem about world peace. The four winning poems were printed on huge greeting cards that Norfolk sent to its four sister cities during the winter holiday season.

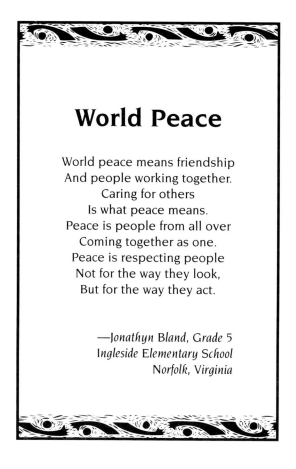

World Peace

World peace means friendship
And people working together.
Caring for others
Is what peace means.
Peace is people from all over
Coming together as one.
Peace is respecting people
Not for the way they look,
But for the way they act.

—*Jonathyn Bland, Grade 5*
Ingleside Elementary School
Norfolk, Virginia

Learn a Language

Ask your teacher about foreign language classes. If your school doesn't offer them, you may be able to enroll in a class through a community education program or through a special language institute in your community. Learning a foreign language is an excellent way to develop an understanding of another culture.

Study a Culture

Classes about different countries can be fun and interesting. Your school or public library may offer some. For example, in Fort Worth, Texas, the sister city committee and the Fort Worth Public Library joined forces to offer a summer reading program. Its theme was "Familiar Faces in Faraway Places." Students who participated learned about Fort Worth's five sister cities while they read for fun.

The sister city program in Fort Worth also held a class in Japanese culture for children ages 6 to 11. For four Saturday mornings, the children joined in activities designed to teach them about Japan. They learned to use chopsticks, make origami figures, and write their names in Japanese characters. They learned about Japanese money and language and made kites and Japanese-style flower arrangements. The class ended with a beautiful tea ceremony presented by the Japanese Society of Fort Worth.

Special Days at School

Ask your teacher or principal to hold a special day at your school to honor your sister city or sister cities. Maybe you would prefer to have an international day to celebrate the many cultures of the world. The day might include presentations, food demonstrations, and activities such as folk dancing. You read about Kameoka Days in Stillwater, Oklahoma. All activities in the schools of Stillwater were about Japan for that one day. To prepare for the special day, you and your classmates could learn some facts about the country or countries and make a presentation.

Other Programs

Sister Cities International offers several programs for young people. If you contact SCI, you can learn more about them. A good place to start might be the National Youth Program, which works to motivate young people to become active participants in sister city programs.

SCI offers several scholarships as well. The Eisenhower Scholarships support international students in their studies at colleges in or near a United States sister city. The Kanazawa Scholarship Program helps young adults between the ages of 18 and 35 develop their careers through on-the-job training. The program matches companies throughout the world with young businesspeople of all nationalities.

You Can Make a Difference

No matter what you do, remember that you can make a difference. You alone can contribute to international understanding. In 1982, a 10-year-old girl from the United States, Samantha Smith, wrote a letter to Yuri Andropov, then premier of the Soviet Union. At that time, the possibility of war existed between the Soviet Union and the United States.

"I have been worrying about the Soviet Union and the United States getting into a nuclear war," Samantha wrote. "Are you going to vote to have a war or not? If you aren't please tell me how you are going to help not have a war."

Samantha became a national hero because she openly expressed the fears of many people, both children and adults. Andropov answered her letter and invited her to visit the Soviet Union. Samantha then spent two weeks in the USSR with her parents, visiting sites and making friends.

Tragically, Samantha and her father were killed in a

Samanatha Smith

plane crash in 1985. Samantha's mother, Jane, then founded the Samantha Smith Center. The center's main activity is a summer camp exchange between youth of the former Soviet Union and the United States.

"Samantha couldn't accept people's inhumanity to one another and hoped that someday soon we would find the way to world peace," said Jane Smith. "I strongly believe that youth exchanges are a critical part in building a world at peace."

Even though people in the United States no longer worry about war with the former Soviet Union, we cannot take peace for granted. People everywhere need to work actively to ensure it. As the 19th-century American writer Ralph Waldo Emerson said, "The only way to have a friend is to be one."

Hands of friendship reach out in this greeting card, designed for a Sister Cities International competition by 17-year-old Merrill Ann White of Charlotte, North Carolina.

You can have a friend—and be one. By getting involved in sister cities and other exchanges, you can learn more about the world. You can discover for yourself the interesting differences among people of various countries and the many ways in which they are alike. Your life will be enriched by your firsthand knowledge of other cultures. But you will gain so much more than knowledge. When you become a friend, you gain a friend. In fact, through sister cities, you can gain friends around the world.

Sister Cities Organizations

The following organizations can give you information about sister cities and other programs that foster international cooperation:

Council of European Municipalities and Regions
41 Quai d'Orsay
75007 PARIS
FRANCE
(1) 45-51-40-01

Represents local and regional interests in Europe, promotes exchanges between local and regional authorities, assists in twinning arrangements, and promotes European unification.

Federation of Canadian Municipalities—International Office
24 Clarence Street
Ottawa, Ontario
CANADA K1N 5P3
613-237-5221

Represents the interests of local governments across Canada; the International Office encourages twinning as a way to offer services to developing countries, develop trade opportunities, exchange information, and promote worldwide peace and prosperity.

Partners of the Americas
1424 K Street NW, Suite 700
Washington, DC 20005
202-628-3300

Private, nonprofit organization engaged in economic and social development and technical training, while fostering friendship and cooperation among countries of the Americas.

People to People International
501 East Armour Boulevard
Kansas City, MO 64109
816-531-4701

A voluntary effort of private citizens to promote international understanding.

Youth activities: High School Student Ambassador Program, Initiative for Understanding (travel to former Soviet Union), Collegiate Ambassador Program, Pen Pal Program

Perhaps Kids Meeting Kids Can Make a Difference
380 Riverside Drive
New York, NY 10025
212-662-2327

Works toward peace, social justice, and understanding among children in the United States, the former Soviet Union, and other countries.

Youth activities: International Children's Summit, pen pal program

Samantha Smith Center
9 Union Street
Hallowell, ME 04347
207-626-3415

Dedicated to fostering international cooperation, understanding, and communications between families and communities in the former Soviet Union and the United States.

Youth activities: Youth Camp Exchange, Pen-Pal Help

Sister Cities International
120 South Payne Street
Alexandria, VA 22314
703-836-3535

Private, nonprofit organization that fosters better international cooperation and understanding through sister city relationships between cities in the United States and other nations.

Youth activities: National Youth Program, Young Artist Program, International Youth Exchange, Eisenhower International Scholarship Program

Wisconsin Coordinating Council on Nicaragua
P. O. Box 1534
Madison, WI 53701
608-257-7230

A nonprofit educational organization that works to develop cooperative programs between individual citizens and citizen groups in the United States and Nicaragua.

Pen Pal Organizations

The following organizations can help you find a pen pal:

Gifted Children's Pen Pals International
166 East 61st Street
New York, NY 10021

International Pen Friends
P. O. Box 290065
Brooklyn, NY 11229

Perhaps Kids Meeting Kids Can Make a Difference
see previous listing

Samantha Smith Center
see previous listing

Student Letter Exchange
630 Third Avenue
New York, NY 10017

World Pen Pals
1694 Como Avenue
St. Paul, MN 55108

Index

Acknowledgments

Photographs reproduced with permission of: Sister Cities International, pp. 6, 22, 84, 89; Steve Feinstein, p. 8; World Cup USA, Chad Dufalt, p. 9; Joseph Armbruster, ©1990, pp. 10, 18 (top), 18–19 (bottom), 34; Courtesy of Amy Bunting, p. 13, 15; Connie Bickman, pp. 16, 61; Ron Wixman, p. 17; Mark Anderson, p. 37; The Children's Museum, Boston, p. 41; Courtesy of the City of Kameoka, p. 43, 45; Courtesy of John Rohrs, Sister Cities Project, Stillwater, OK/Kyoto, Japan, pp. 44, 45; NOVOSTI/SOVOTO, p. 48; Courtesy of Boulder-Dushanbe Sister Cities, p. 49; Nancy Hoyt Belcher, p. 52; Courtesy of Amesbury for Africa, Dr. Mark Bean, pp. 53, 55; Tom Moran, p. 56 (top); Neighbors Abroad of Palo Alto, p. 56 (bottom); City of Witten, Germany, p. 60; City of Portland Oregon Visitors Association, p. 64; Courtesy of Greenville Sister Cities International, pp. 68, 69; Courtesy of Tom Rieke, pp. 73, 75, 76 (both), 77; Courtesy of Mitake Holloman, p. 80; Courtesy of the authors, p. 83; Courtesy of Norfolk Sister Cities, p. 85; Courtesy of The Samantha Smith Center, p. 88.

Front cover: Elaine Little (lower left); Leslie Fagre (upper left); World Bank (upper right); American Lutheran Church (lower right). Back cover: Sister Cities International, courtesy of Richard Oakland.